JADV-PIC OEL
A tale of two mommies /
Oelschlager, Vanita
921647

D0687171

VE MAR 2012

LU JUN 2012

RE JUL 2015

SU OCT 2016

A Tale of Two Mommies

by Vanita Oelschlager

illustrations Mike Blanc

VanitaBooks, LLC

I dedicate this book to Michelle, Cheryl and Nico, and as always to all my grandchildren.

Vanita Oelschlager

ACKNOWLEDGMENTS
Mike Blanc
Kristin Blackwood
Kurt Landefeld
Paul Royer
Sheila Tarr
Jennie Levy Smith
Elaine Mesek
Michelle
Cheryl
Nico
Kelly Fogel
Carolyn Brodie
Michael Olin-Hitt
Steve Cosby

A Tale of Two Mommies
VanitaBooks, LLC
All rights reserved.
© 2011 Vanita Oelschlager
No part of this book may be reproduced, stored in or introduced into a retrieval system, or transmitted, in any form or by any means (electronic, mechanical, photocopying, recording or any other system currently known or yet to be invented) – except by reviewers, who may quote brief passages in a review to be printed in a newspaper or print or online publication – without the express written permission of both the author and the illustrators, as well as the copyright owner of this book, Vanita Oelschlager. The scanning, uploading, and distribution of this book via the Internet or via any other means without the prior permission of the publisher is illegal and punishable by law. Please do not participate in or encourage electronic piracy of copyrighted materials. Your support of the author's and illustrator's rights is appreciated.

Text by Vanita Oelschlager
Illustrations by Mike Blanc
Design by Mike Blanc and Jennie Levy Smith, Trio Design & Marketing Communications
Printed in China
Hardcover Edition ISBN 978-0-9826366-6-4 Paperback Edition ISBN 978-0-9826366-7-1

www.VanitaBooks.com

A Tale of Two Mommies

by Vanita Oelschlager

illustrations Mike Blanc

VanitaBooks, LLC

If you have a momma and a mommy,
who fixes things when they break?

Oh, *Mommy* has
all the tools.
There's nothing she
can't fix or make.

Who's your mom for riding a bike?

And who's your mom for flying a kite?

Momma's the one for riding a bike.

She's also the one for flying a kite.

Which mom is there when you want to go fishing?

Which mom helps out when Kitty goes missing?

Mommy helps when I want to go fishing.

Both mommies help when Kitty goes missing.

Glub, Glub, Glub? (Translation:)

Who's your mom when you set up your campsite?

Who's your mom for scary faces with flashlights?

Mommy helps to set up the campsite.

Momma makes great scary faces with a flashlight.

Which mom coaches your T-ball team?

Which mom's there when you've had a bad dream?

Mommy is the coach of my T-ball team.

Both mommies are there when I've had a bad dream.

Who’s your mom when you’re climbing a tree?

Who's your mom when you scrape your knee?

Momma helps me climb a tree.

Both moms help when I skin my knee.

Who empties your pockets at the end of the day?

Who teaches you what's the polite thing to say?

I empty my own pockets at the end of the day.

Both moms know what's the polite thing to say.

Does either mom like to pet a snake?

Which mom likes to bake some cake?

Neither mom really likes a snake.

But *Mommy* likes to bake the cakes.

Who's your mom for making beans and rice?

Who helps you out when your friends aren't nice?

Mommy makes me beans and rice.

And she also helps when my friends aren't nice.

Which mom sorts your collection of rocks?

Which mom is there when you just need to talk?

I'm the one who sorts my rocks.

Of course, *both* moms are there when I need to talk.

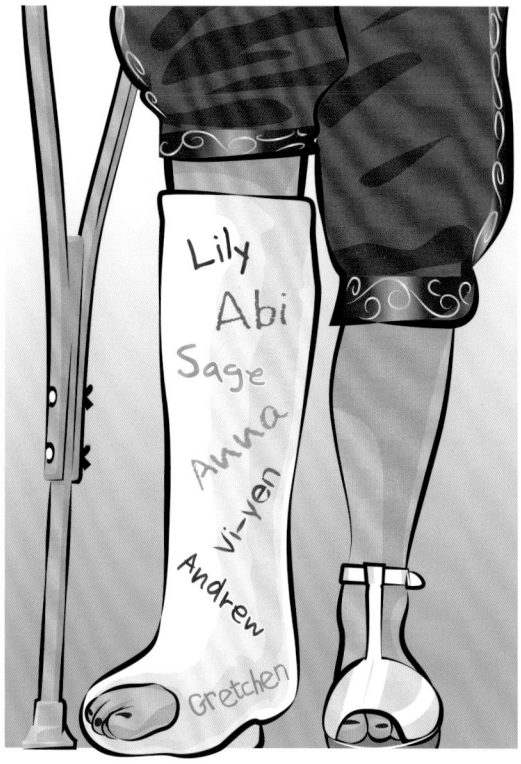

Vanita Oelschlager is a wife, mother, grandmother, philanthropist, former teacher, current caregiver, author and poet. A graduate of Mount Union College in Alliance, Ohio, she now serves as a Trustee of her alma mater and as Writer in Residence for the Literacy Program at The University of Akron. Vanita and her husband Jim were honored with a *Lifetime Achievement Award* from the National Multiple Sclerosis Society in 2006. She was the Congressional *Angels in Adoption* award recipient for the State of Ohio in 2007 and was named *National Volunteer of the Year* by the MS Society in 2008. Vanita was also honored in 2009 as the *Woman Philanthropist of the Year* by the Summit County Chapter of the United Way.

Mike Blanc is a life-long professional artist who has illustrated countless publications for both corporate and public interests worldwide. Accomplished in traditional drawing and painting techniques, he currently works almost exclusively in digital media. His first book, *Francesca*, was written by Vanita Oelschlager and published in 2008. Their second collaboration, *Postcards from a War*, followed in 2009. Additional titles with Vanita are *Bonyo Bonyo, The True Story of a Brave Boy from Kenya*, and *A Tale of Two Daddies*, both co-illustrated with associate artist Kristin Blackwood.

About the Art

The artwork for *A Tale of Two Daddies* was developed and produced in four steps.

First: The characters were established through pencil sketches that were refined in editing sessions as the story developed. Drawings for each page were scanned into computers to form templates.

Second: The artist used Adobe® Illustrator® vector-editing software to plot each shape needed to build the illustration using curve and corner points that were then adjusted, converting each sketch to a computerized version.

Third: Every shape was then assigned a color attribute based on the book's color palette.

Fourth: The template was discarded and the image was fine-tuned with softening effects and transparency. Once complete, the illustrations were gathered and placed into the book design for the finished work: *A Tale of Two Mommies*.

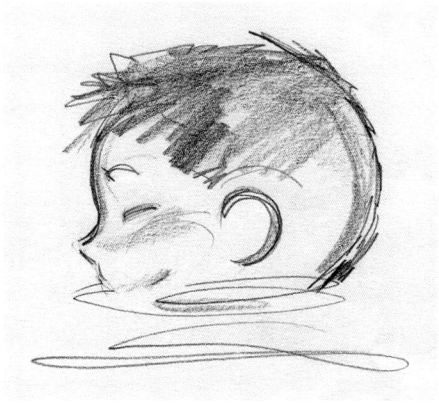

Step 1

Step 2

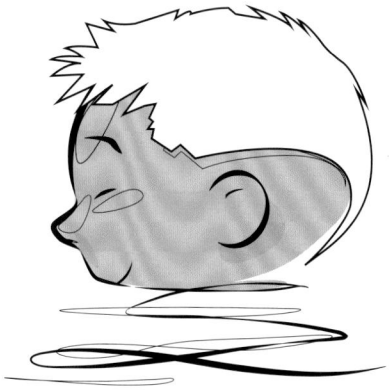

Step 3

Step 4

Profits

All net profits from this book will be donated to charitable organizations, with a gentle preference toward those serving people with my husband's disease – multiple sclerosis.

Vanita Oelschlager

VanitaBooks, LLC